A BIRD ON MY HAND

MAKING FRIENDS WITH CHICKADEES

Mary Bevis

illustrations by
Consie Powell

Raven Productions, Inc. Ely, Minnesota

*To my mother, Helen Palmquist, who shared her love
of chickadees with her grandchildren, and to those
grandchildren: Randy, Ben, David, Matthew, Nels, Ibet,
and especially Karen, whose artwork inspired this story.*
　　　　-- M.B.

For Beckie
　　　　-- C.B.P.

*The illustrations are hand-colored woodblock prints.
The art on the title page is adapted from a crayon drawing made in
1971 by the author's daughter, Karen Bevis Tamte, at age 5.*

Published July 2014 by
Raven Productions, Inc.
P.O. Box 188, Ely, MN 55731
218-365-3375
www.RavenWords.com

Text © 2014 by Mary Bevis
Illustrations © 2014 by Consie Powell

Library of Congress Cataloging-in-Publication Data

Bevis, Mary, 1939-
 A bird on my hand : making friends with chickadees / by Mary Bevis ; illustrated by Consie Powell.
    pages cm
 Summary: On a visit to Gramma's lake house, a child practices feeding sunflower seeds to chickadees by hand.
Includes facts about chickadees.
 ISBN 978-0-9883508-9-2 (hard cover library binding : alk. paper) -- ISBN 978-0-9883508-8-5 (softcover : alk. paper)
[1. Chickadees--Fiction. 2. Birds--Fiction. 3. Grandmothers--Fiction.] I. Powell, Consie, illustrator. II. Title.
PZ7.B46853Bir 2014
[E]--dc23
　　　　　　　　2014007674

Printed in Canada
10 9 8 7 6 5 4 3 2 1

ENVIRONMENTAL BENEFITS STATEMENT

Raven Productions Inc saved the following
resources by printing the pages of this book on
chlorine free paper made with 10% post-consumer
waste.

TREES	WATER	SOLID WASTE	GREENHOUSE GASES
2	539	36	99
FULLY GROWN	GALLONS	POUNDS	POUNDS

Environmental impact estimates were made using the Environmental Paper Network
Paper Calculator 3.2. For more information visit www.papercalculator.org.

We're on our way to Gramma's.
Fireflies flicker and flash
along the road.

Around her cabin, my Gramma is known as the Chickadee Lady. "Chickadee-dee, come to me," she calls. "Chickadee-dee," answer the tiny birds high in the forest pines. One by one, the birds eat from her hand until the sunflower seeds are gone.

Last summer Gramma held my hand steady while I fed them. "To make sure you don't pull away and scare my birds," she said.

"Gramma, we're here!"
I run to the closet and grab
a fistfull of seeds. Out the door
I fly. This summer, I'm going
to feed the chickadees myself.

Into the darkness I call,
"Chickadee-dee,"
holding my hand flat
like Gramma does.
"Chickadee-dee,"
I call again.

"What *are* you doing?"
Gramma asks from behind
the screen door.
"I'm feeding the birds,"
I answer.

"Not at night. They're
roosting. They're all sleeping
in the woods."

Just before sunup
the birds wake me.
The woods are alive
with songs and calls.
Quicker than I can
say chickadee,
I jump out of bed,
grab the bucket of
seeds, and race
through the door.

"Don't scare my birds,"
Gramma orders. "It took
me a long time to build
their trust."
"Dee-dee-dee," the
chickadees call to each other.
          "Chickadee-dee-dee."

"Chickadee-dee,"
I call in my best
bird voice.
I hold out my hand.
"Breakfast!"

One little bird lands
on the railing.

Hold still,
I remind myself.
*Don't scare
Gramma's birds.*

But the
chickadee
takes a seed from
the feeder. Many
others come, but not
one bird takes my seed.
"What did I do wrong?"
I ask Gramma.
"Not a thing. It
just takes time
before they'll
trust you."

Gramma whistles a soft chickadee call. The birds fly in, dipping up and down. One lands on her hand, takes a seed, and flies away. Another zips down, and then another, until I lose count.

One tiny chickadee watches me carefully. I stand as still as a tree trunk, my arm like a branch and seed in my hand.

"Chickadee-dee-dee," I softly call. "Don't be afraid of me." The bird tilts its head and looks me over.

Can I trust you? I wonder. *You won't peck at my hand?* The chickadee flies right toward me. *Stay still,* I tell myself, but my arm pulls away. The bird flutters by and lands on Gramma's shoulder.

"I'm sorry. I didn't mean to move."

"That's all right. Want me to help?"

"No." I stretch my arm out. "I want to do it myself."

In a flash another chickadee lands on the railing, right next to my hand. I almost pull away. *Stay still,* I tell myself. *Be brave.* I wonder if the chickadee is thinking the same. Tiny black eyes look me over as the bird hops onto the tip of my finger, holding on with scratchy dry claws. The bird chooses a seed and is off with a flutter. It perches on a branch, holds the seed between its toes, taps the shell open, and eats the soft morsel inside.

"I did it. I really fed it!"

"Quiet now," Gramma warns. "Another's coming."

Three more birds eat from my hand. Then my seeds are gone and I put my hand down.

"That's right," says Gramma.

"If you offer an empty hand, you'll disappoint the birds and they'll stop coming."

"See you later," I call to the birds. Gramma and I go in to make blueberry pancakes.

Just before lunch, as Gramma and I tie up the fishing boat, the chickadees call again. I'm ready.

"Chickadee-dee-dee, wait for me." I pull a handful of smooth seeds from my pocket and rest my open hand on the railing. I stand very, very still. Right away a spunky chickadee lands on my hand! It takes a seed and flies off. The next bird picks up a seed and drops it back into my hand. It picks up another and another until it finally keeps one.
"You're picky," I say.

I jump when a chickadee flies in from behind me. Its wings nearly brush my cheek. The bird lands on my hand. It has feathers sticking up all over its head.
"I'll call you Scruff."

In flies the smallest
chickadee.
"What a squirt."
A larger fluffy
chickadee chases
Squirt away.
"Dee-dee-dee," it
scolds. "Dee-dee-dee."
"You sure are bossy."
Bossy chooses the
fattest seed.

When Squirt hops back
on my hand, I whisper,
"Littlest chickadee, you
can trust me."

Every day I feed the birds at Gramma's. By the end of the week, I know each one: Spunky, Picky, Scruff, Bossy, and Squirt.

"I don't want to go home," I tell Gramma. "I'll miss my friends. Will Squirt be here next summer?"
"Maybe." She smiles. "Some chickadees live to be ten years old."

"Do you think our city chickadees would eat from my hand?"
"Perhaps," says Gramma, "if you're patient. Put a mitten by your feeder, and keep the palm filled with sunflower seeds until I visit this fall."

"I still don't want to
go home."
Gramma puts her arm
around me. "I don't
want you to leave either.
Our birds will find food,
but who will eat my
blueberry pancakes?"

Before it's time to leave,
I draw a picture of Squirt
eating from my hand.
I tuck the drawing in
Gramma's seed bucket.

Back at home, I fill our feeder with sunflower seeds. Then I put my old wool mitten on the feeding tray and pour more seeds over it. I watch from the window, but no birds come.

In a while I notice one chickadee, then another and another. Soon lots of other birds arrive.

Gramma wouldn't even need to see the birds to know who's around. She'd say, "I hear the cardinal. Oh, you have a robin. Listen to those finches."

Without Gramma, I need a bird book.

Each day I make sure the feeder is full. Sometimes I run outside and offer seeds in my hand, but the birds all fly away.

The days get cooler and the leaves turn red and yellow.

A postcard arrives.

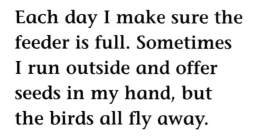

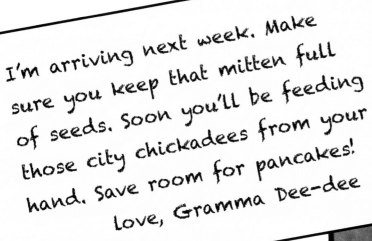

I'm arriving next week. Make sure you keep that mitten full of seeds. Soon you'll be feeding those city chickadees from your hand. Save room for pancakes! Love, Gramma Dee-dee

The feeders are almost empty the day Gramma arrives. "Good," she says. "Better not to have too much seed around when you're trying to hand-feed the birds."

The next morning, after blueberry pancakes, Gramma puts lawn chairs next to the feeder. "Let's chat," she says.

"Chat about what? I just want to feed a chickadee from my hand."

"Patience," says Gramma.

"These city chickadees need to get used to us."

Three times a day we sit by the feeders and the birds fly around us. We talk softly.

"Fall is the perfect time to begin feeding," says Gramma. "The birds are searching for a reliable source of food. When your feeder has seeds every day, they'll come often."

"Will they leave like the robins do?"

"No, they'll be here all winter."

"How will they keep warm?"

"By eating your sunflower seeds."

On the third morning Gramma says, "The
birds know us now. Let's see if they'll trust you."
We take our places next to the empty feeder.
I slip my hand into the mitten and stay very
still. Only my eyes move. The chickadees call
to each other as they flit from bush to tree.
"Chickadee-dee-dee," I softly call.
"Come to me."

One bold chickadee flies down and perches on
the feeder. It looks me over. I stay so still that I
hold my breath.
Finally, the bird
flies to my
mitt and
snatches a seed!

I want to shout!
Instead, I whisper.

"Welcome, Scout."

"Another's coming," says Gramma.
"Quiet," I tease. "Don't scare my birds."

WHICH CHICKADEES LIVE NEAR YOU?
If they come to your feeder, you can teach them to eat from your hand. Here's how:

Put sunflower seeds on a mitten in a feeder you can reach. Sometimes sit quietly nearby. You may talk softly. When the chickadees have been taking seeds from the mitten for a few days and seem accustomed to your presence, take most of the seed from the feeder. Wear the mitten and put seed in your palm. Hold your hand out flat, resting it on the feeder.

When the chickadees come, stay as still as you can. Talk softly to the birds. Don't stare at them, move your hand closer, or try to stop them when they fly away, as those actions could scare them. When you leave the feeder, put more seeds there for the chickadees.

Once the chickadees are comfortable eating from your hand, you don't need to stand so still. When you are comfortable with the birds, you don't need to wear the mitten. The chickadees may fly to you and land on your head or shoulder. Remember to carry seed in your pocket. Then you will be ready when the chickadees come.

BLACK-CAPPED CHICKADEE

CHESTNUT-BACKED CHICKADEE

MOUNTAIN CHICKADEE

MEXICAN CHICKADEE

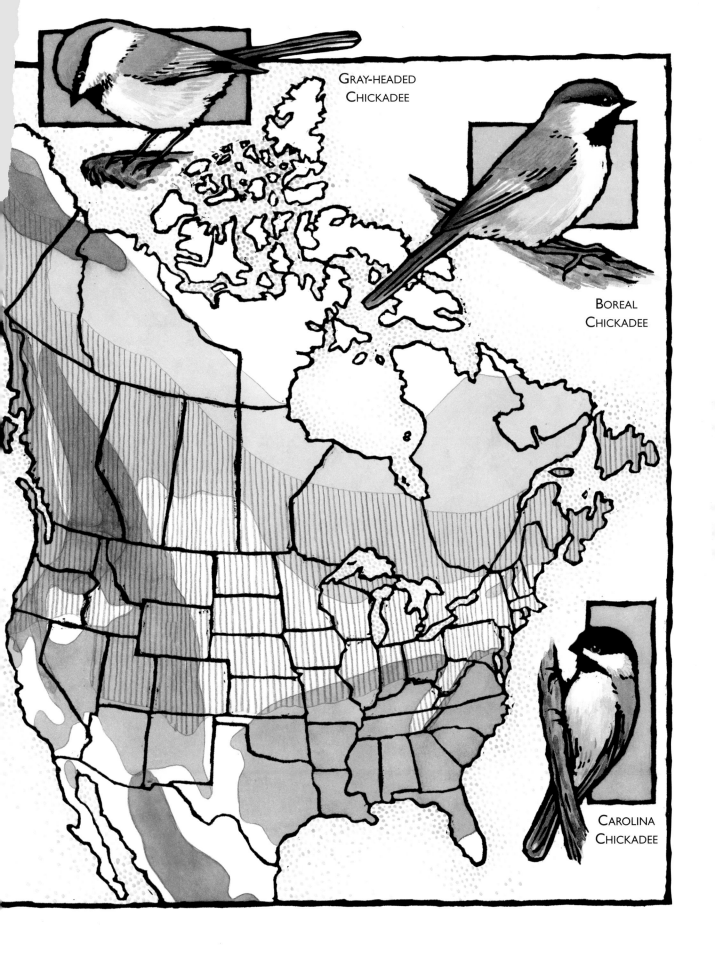

GRAY-HEADED
CHICKADEE

BOREAL
CHICKADEE

CAROLINA
CHICKADEE

CHICKADEE TIDBITS

A chickadee is tiny. It weighs only as much as two quarters.

Although chickadees seem to relish seeds and suet that people provide, they eat many other kinds of food and thrive in wilderness areas where there are no feeders. In warm weather they eat caterpillars, beetles, spiders, insect eggs and larvae, and slugs. In spring they eat the sweet icicles formed by dripping maple sap. In winter they eat seeds and berries. Anytime they have the chance to eat animal fat, such as from a dead deer, they will take advantage of it. Chickadees often eat hanging upside down.

To survive harsh winter weather, chickadees have some remarkable adaptations. Feathers protect them from wind and rain and are their only insulation. Chickadees can drop their body temperature by as much as twelve degrees on cold winter nights to save fuel–like turning down the thermostat in your house. They shiver when they need to warm up. They store food in the fall and remember where it is during winter storms. Although they don't have fat for insulation, their bodies convert the food they eat during the day into fat that is burned at night.

Chickadees make their nests in holes in trees. Usually they improve an existing hole, often using one made by a woodpecker. Both the male and female dig out soft rotten wood to expand the hole. They carry the chips away from the nest site so predators won't detect the nest. Then they add soft material, such as moss and plant fluff. One chickadee was seen pulling a tuft of fur from a dog!

Chickadees usually lay six to eight eggs, which are white with reddish-brown spots. Each egg is about the size of a small jelly bean. Like most birds, chickadees use their nests only when they have babies. They sleep in roosting spots once the young are out of the nest. Most black-capped chickadees roost alone in a small hole in a tree or in dense vegetation.

Chickadees don't migrate and seldom go more than a mile or two from their birthplace unless food is scarce. Their average lifespan is two and a half years, but researchers know of some that have lived to be more than twelve years old.